MW00744155

Dedicated to Mommy, who so luckily got to "live" this book,
and to our little Goosey-Goo, the shining light in our hearts. —A.L.S.

To Doug, Samantha, and Carter —A.C.

Text copyright © 2012 by Alan Lawrence Sitomer
Illustrations copyright © 2012 by Abby Carter

All rights reserved. Published by Disney • Hyperion Books, an imprint of Disney Book Group. No part of this book
may be reproduced or transmitted in any form or by any means, electronic or mechanical, including photocopying,
recording, or by any information storage and retrieval system, without written permission from the publisher.
For information address Disney • Hyperion Books, 114 Fifth Avenue, New York, New York 10011-5690.

Printed in Malaysia
First Edition
3 5 7 9 10 8 6 4 2
H106-9333-5-12218

Library of Congress Cataloging-in-Publication Data

Sitomer, Alan Lawrence.
    Daddies do it different / by Alan Lawrence Sitomer ; illustrated by Abby Carter.—1st ed.
       p. cm.
    Summary: A child relates all the things that Daddy does differently than Mommy, but the most
important thing they do exactly the same.
    ISBN 978-1-4231-3315-5
    1. Father and child—Fiction. 2. Fathers—Fiction. [1. Mothers—Fiction] I. Carter, Abby, ill. II. Title.
PZ7.S6228Dad 2012
[E]—dc22   2010042927

Designed by Tanya Ross-Hughes
Text is set in 16-point Chaloops
Reinforced binding

Visit www.disneyhyperionbooks.com

Daddies
do it different

by Alan Lawrence Sitomer
Illustrated by Abby Carter

DISNEY · HYPERION BOOKS
NEW YORK

When Mommy gets me dressed in
the morning, I look extra cute.

My blouse is clean,
my shoes have style,

and my socks always match my shirt.

But daddies do it different.

Stripes collide with plaids,

my barrettes are crazy crooked,

and sometimes my head
pops through the shirtsleeve!

When Mommy feeds me breakfast,
it's always really yummy.

I sit nicely at the table,
munch a piece of toast,

and we talk about our plans for the day.

But daddies do it different.
We make a fort with waffles,

get syrup on the dog,
and eat cereal straight out of the box!

At the market, Mommy straps me into the cart,
reads lots of different labels,
and uses coupons to save our family money.

But daddies do it different.

He gobbles down free samples,
drives our shopping cart like a race car,

and puts bananas up his nose
to try to make me laugh.

In the kitchen, Mommy teaches me how to mix sauces.

Daddy shows me how to juggle eggs.

When I leave the house with Mommy,
she packs a tasty snack,
brings a bit of juice,
and takes an extra sweater.

But daddies do it different.

He grabs his cell phone,
checks his wallet,
then spends ten minutes trying to find his "stoopid" car keys.

At the park, Mommy puts sunscreen on my face.

Daddy pulls a muscle on the monkey bars.

At birthday parties, Mommy chats with other parents.

Daddy eats three pieces of cake.

When Mommy does her makeup,
she lets me put on blush,

try on her shoes,
and jingle lots of bracelets.

But daddies do it different.
He shows me how to shave,

teaches me to gargle,

then uses gobs of hair gel to give my curls pizzazz.

When Mommy gets her nails done,
I sometimes get mine painted, too.

When Daddy watches Sunday sports, I sometimes see him cry.

Mommy smiles when we play tic-tac-toe.

Daddy gets mad because I whup him.

In the bath, Mommy gets me clean and fresh.
She washes me top to bottom,

I play with my favorite toys,

and when it's time to come out,
she wraps me in a nice, fluffy towel.

But daddies do it different.
A billion bubbles fill the tub,
water floods the floor,
and when we're done, DADDY is just as wet as I am.

At bedtime, Mommy dims the lights,
dresses me in a clean pair of jammies,

and we never forget
to brush my teeth.

But daddies do it different.

With a thousand kooky voices,
Daddy reads me silly stories,

we jump like kangaroos,

and he tickles me so much,
I get crazy-hyper-nuts!

When it's finally time to go to sleep,
Mommy tucks me under my blankie,
gives me a tender kiss,
and tells me just how much she loves me.

And daddies do it . . .

. . . the exact same way.